Quest for the Crown

ELEANOR COOMBE

illustrations by ANDREW SMITH

LOTHIAN
Children's Books

The Faraway Fairies™

For Barbara

A Lothian Children's Book

Published in Australia and New Zealand in 2008
by Hachette Livre Australia Pty Ltd
Level 17, 207 Kent Street, Sydney NSW 2000
Website: www.hachettechildrens.com.au

Text copyright © Eleanor Coombe 2008
Illustrations copyright © Andrew Smith 2008

National Library of Australia
Cataloguing-in-Publication data:

Coombe, Eleanor.
Quest for the crown.

For children.

ISBN 978 0 7344 1039 9 (pbk.).

Special price ed.
For children.

ISBN 978 0 7344 1064 1 (pbk.).

1. Fairies - Juvenile fiction. I. Title. (Series :
Faraway fairies ; 1).

A823.4

Text design by Christa Moffitt, Christabella Designs
and Simon Paterson, Bookhouse
Typeset in 14/20 pt Bembo by Bookhouse, Sydney
Cover design by Christa Moffitt, Christabella Designs
Printed by Midas Printing, China

Hachette Livre Australia's policy is to use papers
that are natural, renewable and recyclable products
and made from wood grown in sustainable forests.
The logging and manufacturing processes are expected
to conform to the environmental regulations
of the country of origin.

Sandy
Wastes

⑦

ains

⑤

rest

①

sand dunes

Fairy
Penguin
Beach

FARAWAY ISLAND

1. Fairy Castle
2. Moon Fairy's Castle
3. Gnome Town
4. Wollemi Lady's
   Secret Valley
5. Bunyip's Pool
6. Goblins' Lair
7. Gryphon
8. The Heart of
   the Island
9. Fafnir's Cave
10. Pinch's Castle

⌒ Goblin Tunnels

Fairy Friends and Foes

Astara: The youngest fairy.

Blaize: The singing fairy.

Dwarf: Mines gold in the High Hills.

Eden: The healing fairy.

Fafnir the dragon: Fairy-eating, jewel-hoarding, bad-tempered dragon.

Goodewin: The gnome-wizard who has a magical crystal ball.

Grim goblins: A band of nasty goblins ruled by Lord Foulweather.

Lord Foulweather: King of the Grim Goblins.

Pooka: A nasty horse-like creature that lives in muddy swamps. Is known to eat fairies.

Puck: The love fairy.

Tom Tot: A happy tiny sunbeam.

Trow: A lonely cake- and wine-loving creature. Lives in a mound of earth.

Water bunyip: A creature who loves clean water and protects her pool.

Wattleman: A tree man.

Yowie: A nasty creature that lives in dark tunnels.

The Stolen Crown

Late one mid-summer's afternoon, a handsome fairy named Blaize, dressed in his best suit and with his hair tied neatly in a ponytail, walked along a forest track. The animals, who knew the fairy well, looked on in surprise. Blaize's face was set in an unusual frown, and they thought it was quite odd he wasn't flying, especially as the guitar he carried looked heavy.

After a few minutes, Blaize stopped beside an ancient gum tree. Happy laughter came from inside. Blaize knocked loudly on the bark. Magically, a door opened and a plump fairy wearing a shimmering blue ball gown greeted him. Her hair tumbled down her back to well below her shoulders.

'Eden,' Blaize greeted his friend wearily, puffed from the long walk, 'are you ready to go to the Great Council?'

'We have hours yet before the meeting!' Eden laughed. 'Come in and wait while I comb Astara's hair.'

Reluctantly, Blaize entered his friends' home. Astara, the youngest fairy, wore a green dress, and her fair hair was long and straight. She sat on a chair waiting for Eden. Eden went to her and began to weave stardust in her hair with her magical golden comb.

Astara smiled at Blaize and said, 'Are you going to sing us one of your famous love songs while we get ready?'

'Not this time,' said Blaize, and his voice sounded so sad the girls stopped what they were doing.

'Is there something wrong?' asked Astara.

'Very wrong,' Blaize replied, 'and I think we had better hurry and leave for the Council now.'

'It's hours away,' Eden persisted. 'We can fly there in seconds once our hair is done.'

'I'm afraid you can't,' Blaize told them. 'The Fairy Queen's crown has been stolen.'

'What? How? Never! That's impossible!' the girls cried.

'The Queen's powers are at their weakest today, because it is time for the Great Fairy Council to elect a new fairy ruler. But now that the enchanted fairy crown has been stolen, we have lost our power to fly.'

'What?' asked Astara, shocked.

'Well, try it,' Blaize replied.

The girls fluttered their wings but nothing happened. In horror they turned to Blaize. 'It took me hours to walk here,' he said.

'You walked!' shrieked Eden. 'We'll never get to the Council in time. I haven't walked anywhere in years.'

'We'd better start out for the Council

immediately if we want to find out what's happening,' Blaize said.

The fairy friends quickly set out for the great fairy castle of Faraway Island. Parrots flew through the air above their heads. 'Fairies walking!' the parrots squawked. 'Now we have seen everything.'

'Our poor Queen!' said Astara. 'What a dreadful way to end such a long and happy reign. How will she crown the new ruler if there is no crown?'

'I really don't know,' replied Blaize, 'but however she does it I hope she will choose someone as lovely as herself. She's been a wonderful ruler for the last thousand years and one of our best fairy queens.'

'I agree,' said Astara. 'She's taught me so many wonderful spells and I've loved working for her. But I think the new ruler might be a man this time, someone like the River Fairy perhaps.'

A stranger's voice interrupted them. 'It might yet be Lord Foulweather on the throne.' A mischievous fairy, with dreadlocks and dressed in red, appeared from behind a large fern tree. Over his shoulder was slung a bow and a quiver of arrows.

'Puck!' cried Eden, stamping her foot. 'Why say such awful things?'

'Because Lord Foulweather has come out of his mountain home and I have just met a frightened bandicoot who saw the goblin's friends spreading ice and cold in the High Hills.'

Just the thought of Lord Foulweather made Astara break out in goosebumps. She shuddered as she remembered his cruel yellow eyes, his dreadful long green teeth, and his long pointy fingernails. It was bad enough he was king of the nasty goblins, but to even suggest he might rule Faraway Island was too terrible to think about.

'Is this another one of your tricks?' asked Astara in total disbelief.

Puck looked very sad. 'I'm not joking,' he answered. 'Not only can't we fly, now Lord Foulweather is trying to rule Faraway Island.'

'We'd better hurry,' said Blaize. 'The Queen will have a plan to fix the problem, I'm sure.'

The Queen's Request

Summer flowers decorated the fairy castle. The polished walls were sprinkled with glittering fairy dust. A thousand torches glimmered in the great hall, one torch for each year of the Fairy Queen's reign.

The beautiful Fairy Queen sat on her crystal throne and watched as the exhausted fairies arrived, rubbed their aching feet and seated themselves.

When the fairies were all settled, the
Queen smiled, waved her translucent lilac
wings and held up one of her hands.
Sparks hovered at her fingertips. The
tinkling conversation stopped and the
fairies fluttered their wings expectantly,
waiting for the Queen to speak.

'As you well know, tonight we *were* going
to celebrate the crowning of a new ruler of
Faraway Island, but with the crown gone, our
plans must change,' said the Fairy Queen.

'Who has taken it?' cried the fairies.

'We think a goblin managed to sneak into the castle. Today is the first day in a thousand years when my fairy powers can't fully protect us. We think Lord Foulweather planned this evil theft over many years and has, sadly, succeeded.'

'We must get the crown back!' cried a fairy. The Queen and all the fairies nodded in agreement.

Once again, the Queen held up her hand for silence. 'I have more bad news for you. Lord Foulweather is much more powerful than ever and he is spreading his cold-hearted ways across Faraway Island. He has sent the horrible hobyahs to spread ice and frost. The trees in the High Hills are dying and the animals are starving. The poor creatures are flocking to our Fairy Forest asking for help. The wicked hobyahs, yowies, willowykes and other nasty beasts are gaining confidence and have begun to leave the High Hills and move towards the towns of the gnomes, elves and pixies.'

A great sigh came from the fairies and the torches flickered and almost went out.

The Queen raised her diamond-tipped sceptre high, so everyone quietened. 'We can't do anything about the goblins until we have our powers restored,' continued the Fairy Queen. 'The crown must be found, and a new ruler must be chosen. The Council has decided that whoever finds the crown and brings it back shall become the next ruler of Faraway Island. We are seeking volunteers to go on the quest.'

The fairies began chattering excitedly at this amazing news. Eden looked at Astara. 'I can't be a champion for the crown,' she whispered. 'I'm just not brave enough. I'm best at weaving hair and mixing lovely spells to fix headaches. I can't imagine walking through the kingdom among the yowies, pookas and hobyahs.' She shuddered at the thought.

'I understand,' said Astara. 'But, although I'm small, I feel I must help.'

'There is no need to ask what the boys will do,' said Eden. 'Look, they are already approaching the throne to offer their help.'

'I can't imagine Puck being king of Faraway Island. He's too naughty,' whispered Astara.

'Yes,' said Eden. 'His love arrows caused a lot of trouble in Gnome Town. He shot the Mayor last week when he was judging a vegetable competition. The mayor fell madly in love with a pumpkin and has been carrying it around and kissing it ever since!' The girls giggled at the thought.

'Still,' said Astara, moving to join the volunteers, 'although he's naughty and doesn't think things through, at least he's trying to help.'

The volunteers lined up beside the Queen and waited for their instructions. The Queen opened a treasure chest beside the throne. 'As our powers are weak, I have collected all the magical jewels from our kingdom. These enchanted gems will help you in times of trouble. I can only hope you will be clever enough to discover their powers and use them wisely.' She reached inside the chest and gave a treasure to each volunteer.

When she came to Puck she chose a ruby. 'A red stone for a fiery fairy,' she said, handing it over. 'I hope you learn some control over yourself, Puck.' The ruby glinted as Puck took his gift and stood to one side.

'For Blaize,' the Fairy Queen said, 'I have a turquoise.'

'Thank you, my lady,' said Blaize, bowing low.

Finally, Astara stood before the Queen.
'My youngest fairy in all the land,' said the
Queen. 'I thought you would stay home.'

'No,' said Astara, 'I'm ready to go out
and search for the crown.'

The Queen looked inside the treasure
chest. 'There is only one left,' she said.
'Lucky last!' She handed Astara a star
sapphire.

The Queen held her sceptre high once
more, then stood and led the way through
the castle to the highest tower. The night
was black and only the Fairy Queen's
sceptre lit the space around them.

'Once the crown is found and we have a
new ruler, we will work to stop the
goblins,' she said. 'I hope your treasures
keep you safe on this dangerous journey,
and you find the crown quickly. We are all
in peril.'

Eden, who had stayed in the hall as the champions were led away, suddenly panicked. 'I didn't say goodbye or wish them luck!' she thought. 'What if something happens to one of them?' She jumped to her feet and ran after her friends.

She arrived at the tower just as the Queen said, 'Let the quest begin,' and raised her sceptre. 'I have summoned a thunderstorm,' she told the brave fairies around her. A great light beamed up from her sceptre and lit the night sky. Dark clouds gathered and a mighty wind buffeted the castle walls. 'The thunderstorm will help scatter you over the kingdom so you don't have to walk. Good luck, my friends!'

With those words, the Fairy Queen stepped back inside the castle, just as Eden ran out. The great storm became fiercer and the wind raged. The fairies spread their wings as the storm gathered them up and scattered them over Faraway Island like dandelion seeds.

A Pixie Party

Unfortunately, the thunderstorm gathered up Eden as she ran out to wish her friends luck on their quest. It whisked her into the air and tumbled her over and over. Her dress covered her head so she couldn't even see where she was going. Finally, a gust of wind tossed her upside down and sent her whirling into a field.

When her dizziness passed, Eden pulled
her dress down and took her magic comb
from her pocket. She tidied her hair. 'If I'm
out here on my own, I'd better look good.
You never know who you'll meet,' she told
herself.

Once she had fixed herself up, she
looked around. There was a trail nearby
that led into a forest. 'Bother,' Eden
thought, 'I wish the path wasn't so dark,

but I want to get back to the castle, so I had best start.'

As she went into the forest, the path became gloomier and gloomier. 'I'll never get home at this rate,' she told herself.

Beneath one of the forest trees a shadow moved. Eden stared at it until her eyes became accustomed to the dark. She soon made out a shabby horse-like creature standing beside the path. 'I'll be able to ride home,' she thought happily.

She strode up to the creature. She noticed it was muddy and its mane was full of pondweed. 'I don't like muddy horses,' muttered Eden. She stepped closer. 'Still, a dirty bottom is better than tired legs.

'Excuse me, but if you are free, I would appreciate it if you could give me a ride,' she called. A nasty red gleam lit the creature's eyes as she approached. 'I have a long way to go,' continued Eden, beginning

to feel nervous, 'and I don't like walking.'
She was just about to reach out and touch
the creature, when a great snort of hot
breath came from its flared nostrils. Eden
jumped back in fear.

'Don't be scared,' hissed the horse-
creature. 'Pooka loves you. Pooka will let
you ride.'

'Pooka!' screamed Eden. 'Pookas eat
fairies!' She turned and ran as fast as she
could, with her wings flapping and her
little feet pounding with all their might.
The pooka ran after her and began to gain
on her. Eden didn't want to be eaten for
dinner. 'It's not fair!' she cried out. 'I should
be home, not out here in the wild!'

The pooka's hot breath steamed down on
her wings and, with her strength failing and
her heart near bursting, she spied a dense
thicket of gum trees. She pelted towards them
and squeezed herself between the trunks.

The pooka was too big to follow. He stopped short, snorted and gnashed his black teeth. 'Come out, little fairy,' he cried. 'Pooka sorry. Pooka not eat you. Pooka like you.' He thought about what he'd said, and then he licked his lips. 'Pooka like you very much!'

'Go away!' screamed Eden.

'Go away indeed,' said a voice from behind Eden. She spun around.

A leafy man emerged from the trees. His beard and hair were covered with golden wattle flowers. The pooka ignored him and tried to squeeze his head between the tightly growing trees to bite at Eden. She cringed back. The leafy man strode forward and smacked the pooka sharply on the nose.

'Ouch,' squealed the pooka. 'Mean old wattleman! Pooka only wants a crunchy fairy.'

'Go back to your home in the High Hills and bother the goblins,' the wattleman ordered.

'Hate goblins,' the pooka answered. 'Ate one few hours ago.'

'What was one doing in my forest?' asked the wattleman.

'Don't know, don't care. Goblin runned fast from fairy castle. Ohhh, it was horrid and dry. I want crunchy, sweet fairy. Give it to me!'

'This is my wood and you are not allowed here. The fairy is my guest. Go away.'

'Pooka wait till fairy come out.'

'Pooka will go!' ordered the wattleman. 'Or I will take my golden flowers and throw them at you.'

'Wattleman wouldn't be so mean,' moaned the pooka. 'Pooka hate golden sunny flowers. Sunny flowers make pooka sick.'

'Then go away,' the wattleman said, and he scooped a bunch of wattle blooms from his beard. 'I have a big bunch . . .'

'Pooka sees them,' screamed the pooka. 'Pooka stinks them. Horrid, horrid, sicky flowers. Pooka hates them and pooka hates

nasty wattleman.' Fearing the flowers would be thrown at him, the pooka turned and galloped away.

'Dear, oh dear,' said the wattleman, shaking his leaves. 'That pooka is brave tonight. So, who have I rescued?'

'I'm Eden. A goblin stole the Fairy Queen's crown, so my friends went off in a thunderstorm and I got caught up in it too −'

'Well, that sounds most odd,' interrupted the wattleman. 'But you *are* a fairy, and I'm sure if you want to get around in a thunderstorm that's fine. And you say the Fairy Queen's crown was stolen by a goblin? How strange. This night is very peculiar indeed.'

'It is,' sighed Eden. 'All I wanted to do was get dressed and go to a nice party, but here I am hurled across the island, hungry and miserable and nearly eaten by a pooka.'

'We have one thing in common,' said the wattleman. 'I was just dressing for a party when you arrived.' The wattleman wove his wattle flowers back into his beard. 'In fact, I think it would be a good idea if you came with me. We can't have the night a total disaster, can we? The pixies are having a big knees-up – lots of singing and dancing.'

Eden thought this was a much better idea than wandering through dark forests and running from pookas, so she agreed.

When they arrived at the party, the wattleman and Eden were greeted enthusiastically by the pixies and were shown where to sit. A band was playing tinkling bells and silver horns, and their joyful songs had the pixies dancing. Everyone wore bright red hats and vivid costumes and they twirled like colours in a kaleidoscope. Lanterns hung from the trees,

and casks of pixie pop and mistletoe milk
leant against the trunks. Golden plates
laden with scrumptious food were carried
to the mushroom tables.

A pixie brought Eden a golden glass of pixie pop. 'Yummmm,' said Eden after guzzling it down in one gulp. 'This is much better than being eaten by a pooka.'

The thought of the pooka frightened her, so she grabbed another glass and drank it down. It wasn't long before she found herself twirling and singing with the pixies. Round and round she went until she was dizzier than she had been in the storm. Every time she stopped to catch her breath, she remembered the pooka and took another glass of pop.

Eden was in the middle of a wild jig, when the music stopped. She spun around and fell against a mushroom. In a flash all the lights went out and the food vanished. 'It is midnight,' the wattleman told her. 'Every mid-summer, the pixies have a party and when they

have danced and eaten all they can, they
go off into the forest and play pranks on
each other.'

'Oh,' said Eden. 'Ooooh.' She grabbed
her tummy. 'I seel very fick.'

'You've had too much pop,' said the
wattleman. 'It can really muddle you up if
you drink too much, and it can make you
burp.'

'Bairies don't furp,' Eden groaned. 'I just
need water.'

'There is a pool just over there.' The
wattleman pointed. 'A water bunyip owns
it, but she doesn't like anyone drinking her
water. Sometimes she demands payment.'

'*Burp.*'

The wattleman raised an eyebrow at Eden
and she went bright red. 'I'd better get that
water.'

'Remember,' the wattleman said, 'she
demands payment.'

'Water's free,' Eden said. 'No old water bunyip is going to worry me.' And, without saying goodbye to the wattleman, Eden wandered off through the trees.

By the time she found the water bunyip's pool she was dreadfully thirsty. Without a thought she knelt and drank. Her head cleared instantly and she felt terrific. 'Ah, that's better,' she sighed and rubbed her tummy. Then she reached into the pool to get some more.

Suddenly, a furry hand clutched hers in a tight grip. Eden tried to pull her hand out of the water, but no matter how much she struggled she was pulled closer to what lay below. Eventually, she lost her balance and fell into the bunyip's pool. When she opened her eyes underwater, she found a furry face and the deepest green eyes she had ever seen glaring back at her. The bunyip was covered in long green fur, which floated out in untidy, knotted streamers around her body. She held Eden at the bottom of the pool, and sang:

'What a naughty fairy, and so greedy,
Not to ask when you are needy.
You guzzle water from my well,
Now I have you in my spell.'

'I'm sorry,' said Eden. 'It's just that I drank too much pixie pop. I didn't think anyone would mind me having some water.'

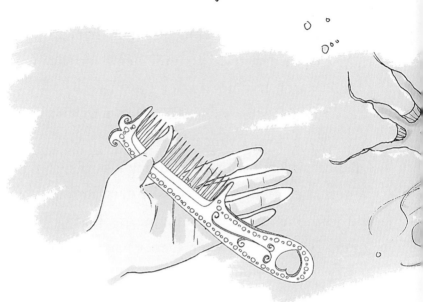

'Water's precious, water's clear,' replied
the singing Bunyip. 'Beautiful water will
cost you dear.'

'I must get home,' said Eden. 'Please let
me go. I didn't mean any harm. Truly, I
said I was sorry.'

'Too late for sorry, fairy bad.

You pay bunyip, or you be sad.'

'What a mess,' said Eden, half-thinking
the bunyip could do with a tidy up and a

good hairstyle. 'I'd love to pay you, but I don't carry any money.'

The water bunyip stared at Eden disbelievingly and sang:

'Not a necklace or a locket?

What have you got in your pocket?'

Eden put her hand in her pocket and pulled out her golden comb. The water bunyip's eyes sparkled at the sight.

'It's my magic comb,' complained Eden.

'And it is my wonderful water,' answered the bunyip.

Eden looked for a way to escape, but the bunyip held her hand tightly and, as if reading her thoughts, waved her other hand through the water and flicked her fingers, *clickity clack*. Dark roots and weeds grew up from the bottom of the pool, snaking through the water and winding around Eden's feet. The water bunyip eyed Eden's comb and waited.

Eden didn't want to be covered in weeds, and she knew that if she continued arguing, things would get worse. Finally, she admitted that she had forgotten her manners and taken something that was not hers. She also realised the bunyip was right because clear healthy water was a great treasure, and she had not valued it or been respectful.

'I will give you the comb on one condition,' said Eden.

'Did I get a condition before you took my water?' asked the bunyip.

'No,' replied Eden, 'I was very rude and greedy. But I would like to comb your hair and get rid of all the knots and weeds and make you beautiful before I give you my comb. I would like to make up for my bad manners.'

The bunyip laughed, and with another click of her fingers the waterweeds disappeared. In a flash, Eden was free. The bunyip took Eden's hand and swam with her to the pool's surface. Eden pulled herself onto a rock and the bunyip sat beside her. Carefully, she teased out all the knots and sticks that were stuck in the bunyip's hair, and braided magic gold dust plaits around her head. When she was finished the bunyip bent over and peered at her reflection.

'This is pretty, bunyip looks sweet.

You made bunyip happy. What a treat.'

Eden bowed her head with respect. 'I was wrong,' she said. 'I have learnt a great lesson. I'm glad I've made you happy.'

The bunyip smiled at Eden and held out her hand.

'I'm glad your little comb is mine,
We'll be friends forever and all time.
Now bunyip has a special gift for you,
So all will know we're friends so true.'

Without another word, the bunyip dived
beneath the water, and seconds later she
returned with a wonderful jewelled cup.
She held the cup out to Eden.

'Bunyip knows the times are bad,
Many animals are very sad.
Give this cup to Fairy Queen,
Always from it will come water clean.
One drop will stop a curse or spell,
Fix a poison, cure the unwell.
When you get home, you will know
This cup's more valuable than any comb.'

'The Fairy Queen will love this cup,'
said Eden. 'She will be very honoured to
have such a gift.'

'You can use it too,' said the bunyip, and
her smile lit up the air between them.

Then she turned and slipped under the
water, not leaving one ripple to show she
had been there.

'You were lucky,' said the wattleman,
approaching Eden. 'I saw what happened.'

'I *was* rather rude,' said Eden.

'Blame the pixie pop,' the wattleman
said. 'I know the bunyip well, and she likes
fairies, but she has her rules. I also know
the cup has wonderful powers. I wonder if
you could stay for a few days near the
pixie village? There are some animals and
plants that could do with some good magic
from your cup.'

Eden looked at the cup, then up at the
night sky. There were pookas around and
the new ruler of Faraway Island had not
yet been chosen. It was a long way to walk
home. 'I will stay till I can fly,' she said. 'I
think I can do lots of good work till then.'

A Song of Slumber

Blaize was buffeted across Faraway Island until his ponytail caught on the branches of a tree and he was dragged from the clouds. He twisted around, grabbed hold of the tree, pulled himself to safety and untangled his hair. Behind him the tree clung to a rugged rock-strewn ledge.

He climbed down from the tree but there was only a high cliff behind him and more of the cliff below. He was stuck on a ledge on the side of High Mountain and he couldn't get down. He decided to play his guitar while he thought about what to do next. He strummed a few notes and was rewarded as the tune echoed among the rocks and returned to him tenfold.

As his music echoed over the cliff face, a door opened in the rocks. A long-bearded dwarf stood in the doorway. 'Who's playing ting-tang in the night and annoying me while I try to work?' roared the dwarf.

Behind the dwarf Blaize noticed a mighty forge and a great pot of molten gold bubbling in a vat. 'I'm Blaize,' he replied. 'Will you tell me how to get down from the mountain?'

The dwarf pulled a large handkerchief from his pocket and mopped his brow. 'I

don't like visitors, not even fairies,' he replied. 'You can't go through here – it's private! I've got rings and swords to forge, and the fing-fang fire will go out if you keep me any longer. So, unless you use your wings, you'll have to go down through the yowie's cavern.'

'Could you show me the way?' Blaize asked, amazed at how rude dwarfs could be.

'*Hhhrrumph!*' groaned the dwarf, and pointed to a black chasm between the rocks. 'Go!' he ordered. 'You can't miss it – it's the only cave around.' Without another word, he turned and slammed his door.

Blaize felt his way along the chasm until he found an even darker tunnel. The tunnel wound steadily downhill and a stale breeze pulled at Blaize's clothing. He crept silently down the tunnel until a voice came to him. The voice sounded cruel and crackly and was singing:

'Yowie, yowie, yowie, yooo,
I've caught something bright and new,
Something hot and hard to chew.'

Blaize followed the voice until a bright light became visible ahead. The light led him to a partially open door. Cautiously, Blaize peered through the gap in the doorway and found a sparsely furnished room. A treasure chest was against one wall and jewelled necklaces, rings and brooches spilled onto the floor. Blaize arched his head around the door to see more.

Without warning, rough hands grabbed him and dragged him into the room. 'Yowwwieeee!' cried the yowie as his strong arms tightened their grip. The yowie slapped the floor of the cave with large feet, and roared with delight. His tiny eyes squeezed shut in happiness. 'Yowwwwie!' he yelled again. 'Look, look! I have caught a goody-two-shoes fairy.'

The yowie pulled Blaize to the corner of the room and took a long chain from the wall. One end of the chain had an iron collar and the other was fastened to the rock. Blaize flinched as the iron collar was padlocked around his neck. He knew that iron was the one mineral that no fairy could escape from. He was trapped.

The yowie took a moment to relish his catch, and Blaize stared at him. The yowie wore a skirt of dead leaves and an iron chain with a key around his neck.

'Never eaten a fairy before,' the yowie chortled. 'Does one fry his wings or stew them?'

Blaize wondered who the yowie was talking to.

'You probably have never seen a fairy before,' continued the yowie, 'for they usually come out at night.'

'I have,' said a tinkling voice. 'I've seen them playing in the flowers.'

Blaize looked around the room again, but no one could be seen.

'Do you think I should eat it raw?' asked the yowie.

'Oh, no, not raw,' said the voice. 'They're very old and tough. They need to be boiled for hours and then they're exquisitely delicious.'

'Oh, bother,' sighed the yowie. 'And how do you expect me to do that? I'll need wood and a pot.'

'You best go into the forest then,' tinkled the voice.

'Do I kill it first?'

'No! Fairies are hard to kill. First you must light a fire to boil the pot. Then you have to cover the fairy in diamonds – diamonds make fairies sing. You can only kill a fairy while it's singing.'

'Is that *so*?' asked the yowie.

'Would I lie to you? It has to sing, otherwise it will disappear when you kill it and all your work will be for nothing.'

'Right! Then I'd better be off. Soonest done, soonest fed,' said the yowie, and he stomped off to find wood.

'So, Blaize,' said the voice. 'You're lucky I'm here, or you'd be dead by now.'

'How do you know my name?' cried Blaize in surprise.

'I've seen you and heard all about you,' said the voice. 'Shade your eyes and look up.'

Blaize did as he was told. Hanging from the ceiling was a lantern. Inside, trapped against the glass, was a tiny glowing man.

'A sunbeam!' exclaimed Blaize.

'Tom Tot is my name – the yowie caught me yesterday. I was flying along lighting the woods, when my light fell on a mirror. My light bounced back and blinded me. I stopped to rub my eyes and the next thing I knew I was being scooped up in this lantern and ended up here.'

'How will we get out?' asked Blaize.

The sunbeam laughed. 'Luckily yowies are very stupid. Once I recognised you, I knew you could save us. You see, one morning I came to Gnome Town and, as I passed the Mayor's house, I heard the end of one of your love songs. All the gnome men were asleep, but the ladies were wide awake and enchanted by your voice.' The sunbeam leapt up and down in the lantern as he spoke. 'That day, the woods were full of lovesick gnome girls plucking daisies and asking if you loved them, or if you didn't, and tossing the petals around willy-nilly. Those who weren't plucking daisies were kissing frogs, hoping they'd turn into handsome princes. I tell you, I got quite sick of hearing Blaize this and Blaize that, and I couldn't wait to get back home that night. But I'm glad to see you now.'

'I'm sorry,' laughed Blaize. 'I understand now why you told the yowie I had to sing. Should I sing him to sleep or make him fall in love?'

'To sleep, of course,' said Tom Tot. 'But I will also fall asleep and my light will go out, so that is why you'll need a fire to see what you're doing. You must take the key from the yowie's neck and undo the padlock around your neck.'

'And the diamonds?'

'Just a bonus for all the trouble the yowie has caused us,' giggled the sunbeam.

It wasn't long before the two friends heard the flip-flapping of the yowie's feet and a great grunting and groaning as he puffed his way into the cavern. He entered the room with a load of wood.

When the yowie had a fire flickering, he went to the treasure chest, sorted through all his jewels and began to drape Blaize with diamonds until he glittered in the firelight.

'Now sing a song!' ordered the yowie.

Blaize took his guitar into his arms and began to sing soft sleepy words of fairy magic. The yowie's eyes began to droop and soon he fell fast asleep at Blaize's feet. At the same time Tom Tot nodded off and his light went out.

In the firelight, Blaize quickly freed himself and took the lantern containing his

friend. He walked a long way from the yowie's door before opening the lantern and shaking the sunbeam awake. Tom Tot flew out. 'Lovely song,' he said. 'Now let me light our way home.'

Just as dawn arrived, they reached the forest. 'I haven't managed to find the crown,' Blaize said sadly.

'But you have a fortune fit for a king!'

'Yes, I will take these diamonds to the Fairy Queen before I set out again on my quest for the crown. But it's a very long walk back to the castle.'

As he spoke, a dirty horse walked up the path towards them. 'I carry fairy home,' said the horse in a syrupy voice. 'I love fairy.' The horse smiled and showed his long black teeth.

Blaize put his hand in his pocket and leant over to Tom Tot. 'The Fairy Queen gave me this present,' he whispered, and showed the turquoise to his friend. Tom Tot smiled as Blaize held the jewel out towards the pooka. The horse reared on his hind legs at the sight of the stone and tried to run away, but the turquoise held him in its spell.

'How clever,' said Tom Tot. 'I never really believed the old story that turquoise could tame any horse.'

The pooka gnashed his teeth and bucked at the words, but Blaize leapt upon his back. 'Fly me to the castle,' he ordered. The pooka snorted and tried to bite Blaize's feet, but Blaize held the stone high and its blue light shone on the pooka and kept him quiet.

'Mean tricksy fairy!' muttered the pooka, and he jumped into the air and flew Blaize towards the castle. Tom Tot flew with them, casting his light over the land.

At the gates of the castle, the pooka stopped. Blaize knew he couldn't just leave him to run off and hunt other creatures, so while he was on the pooka's back he wove the turquoise into his mane. Then he whispered a wonderful fairy spell:

'Turquoise stone, oh so old,

Keep the pooka in your hold.

Teach him warmth and wisdom right,

May people smile at the pooka's sight.

With time, let him be good and kind,

And an honest heart let him find.'

Then Blaize jumped down and waved to Tom Tot. 'Goodbye and good luck,' he called as the sunbeam flew off to do his work.

'Goodbye and bad luck,' grouched the pooka. He lunged out with his teeth and tried to bite Blaize. In return, Tom Tot gave the pooka a great smack on his rump with a hot bolt of sunlight, which made the shaggy fur on the pooka's bottom smoke. The pooka leapt with fright and sped to the nearest waterhole to soak his rump.

Strangely, as he sat in the waters, the pooka began to feel an unusual warmth enter his heart and a happy smile creep onto his face. Stranger still, he caught himself chewing grass while he waited for his bottom to cool.

A Fiery Encounter

Puck and Astara almost collided in the storm. Astara had a brief glimpse of Puck as he hurtled past her. Below them, a gnome was out for a mid-summer's night stroll. He hadn't been expecting a storm so he had worn his special cloak. 'Bother,' said the gnome when he noticed the clouds gathering overhead.

'I don't want my cloak ruined.' He ran towards the shelter of a big tree.

Astara and Puck, circling high above, were suddenly caught in a thunderbolt. It shot them from the clouds and rocketed them to land. It catapulted Astara right into the gnome, and she knocked him flat, just as the thunderbolt shot past him and blasted the tree.

The gnome waited till the leaves and twigs from the tree stopped falling before pulling himself to his feet. 'I was silly to run under a tree in a thunderstorm,' he thought. 'I was lucky I wasn't killed.' He straightened his cloak and, as he did so, he discovered Astara lying in the grass. He realised the fairy must have knocked him down just before the lightning hit, and had probably saved his life. He knelt down and patted Astara's hand.

Astara slowly opened her eyes, then stood up and rubbed her ears. As she recovered, the gnome shook the twigs off his cloak. It rippled with a sparkling mauve light, as if all the stars in the sky had been woven into its cloth.

'You have a beautiful cloak,' Astara said, gathering her wits.

'It was given to me by your Fairy Queen,' said the gnome proudly. 'I've had it for more than 700 years.' Astara looked intrigued. 'Yes,' continued the gnome, 'I was a great help to her when Fafnir the dreadful dragon attacked your castle and demanded all your treasures.'

'I remember,' Astara replied. 'I was quite small then. I remember looking out my window and seeing Fafnir's long tail whipping the clouds and his flames scorching the bricks on my balcony.'

'I helped your queen find a spell in the Dragon Law Book,' said the gnome. 'We created a wonderful illusion of a giant knight with a terrible sword. Fafnir was so frightened he turned blue and bolted back into his lair.'

'The story is still told about how you helped us,' said Astara. 'You must be Goodewin, the gnome-wizard.'

The wizard poked his chest out in pride and chuckled. 'So you know who I am, but what are you doing hurtling around in a thunderstorm?'

Astara quickly related the tale of the stolen crown and how none of the fairies could fly until it was found.

'I think I can help,' said the wizard. 'Especially as you saved my life. If we toddle back to my place I can look in my crystal ball, think up a spell, and see where that crown might be hidden.'

Meanwhile, Puck had also been dragged from the sky by the thunderbolt, but had landed softly in a pile of hay left out by one of the gnome farmers. He had bounced to the ground and begun to walk, but hadn't gone far before he heard the wizard and Astara talking. 'If we find the goblin, then we'll find the crown,' the wizard was saying. Puck knew he had to follow Astara and Goodewin to the wizard's house.

When Astara and the wizard were inside, Puck tiptoed to a window and watched as they went to a large desk and Goodewin opened a spell book. Beside the book was a crystal ball set on a tripod of gold. The wizard opened the spell book, flicked through the pages and then picked up a tiny bottle from a bench. He shook the bottle and opened it, then allowed a glimmering rainbow drop of fluid to fall onto his hands. Finally, he and Astara leant over the crystal ball, which flickered with mysterious lights.

'A goblin has certainly stolen the crown,' said Goodewin. 'See him run through the forest with it?' He paused.

'Oh, look,' said Astara, 'there is a pooka in his way.' Astara and the wizard grimaced then grasped.

'Tut, tut,' said the wizard, 'that was not a pretty sight . . . and now the crown is on the ground, just lying in the forest. No, wait...' and the wizard's voice dropped so low that Puck could hear no more. He crept back into the leafy shadows of the garden and waited till the wizard's door opened and Astara stepped outside.

'Thank you,' she said, as she waved farewell to the wizard. 'If I find the crown, I will send you a gorgeous hat to match your cloak.'

The gnome-wizard laughed heartily. 'That would be very nice.'

Astara set off through the forest, unaware that Puck was following her. She weaved swiftly through the trees and Puck struggled to keep her in sight. Eventually, she came to a large mound of tightly packed earth. As she approached the mound, she began to dance, and as she twirled she sang a spell:

'Hobhole muckle moor.

Open, open secret door.'

Quick as a flash a hatch appeared, imbedded in the earth. Astara lifted a latch and went inside. Puck raced to follow her.

Astara carefully walked down a flight of stairs to an untidy room. Scraps of food, spilt goblets of wine and partially eaten cake lay scattered over a large table. A trow was sleeping on the floor, his stomach bulging under his coat, his hands covered in sticky cake. His long nose wiggled as he snored and his hair was wild and wiry.

Astara knew trows were not dangerous, they loved feasting and treasure. And, as her eyes travelled around the room, she spied the crown not far from the sleeping trow's hand. From the crystal ball, she knew the trow had found the Fairy Queen's crown lying on the forest floor after the pooka had gobbled up the goblin. The trow had innocently brought the treasure home. She could not believe her luck as she picked up the crown.

Puck stood on the trow's stairway as
Astara lifted the crown. 'Astara is much too
lucky,' he thought. 'This is a competition
and a competition is a bit like a war, and
all is fair in love and war,' he reasoned. A
naughty smile crept across his face and he
just couldn't help himself. He reached into
his quiver, brought out one of his love
arrows, fitted it to his bow, and fired. The
arrow zipped through the air and hit
Astara's arm.

Unfortunately, at that moment Astara had been looking at the trow and she now clasped her heart and gazed adoringly at him. The crown slipped from her hands and was forgotten – Astara cared for nothing now except her trow.

Puck, on the other hand, felt it was his duty to keep the crown safe. As quiet as a shadow, he slid into the room. He had a lasting vision of Astara as she leant down to kiss the trow. A chuckle burst from his lips as he raced up the stairs with the crown.

Just as Astara was about to press her lips to the trow's cheek, Puck's arrow caught on the trow's coat and pulled free. Astara awoke from the magic. The trow continued to snore and Puck's laughter echoed in her ears. She noticed the tiny arrow in the trow's coat and a red mark on her arm.

'Puck!' she cried. 'Puck has tricked me!' She ran up the stairs and managed to catch

a glimpse of the naughty fairy as he ran
into the forest. She followed him.

As Puck ran, he realised he was getting
closer to the High Mountain. He paused
for a moment. 'It would be nicer to fly,'
he thought. 'If I have the crown, then I
should have all my powers back.' He
put the crown on his head and flapped
his wings. Nothing happened.

'Perhaps I must get back to the castle
and be crowned by the Council before I
can fly,' Puck thought. 'If that's the case,
I'd better get home as fast as possible.

The quickest way will be over High Mountain.'

What Puck didn't know was that the crown would never work its magic on a person who was not completely honest.

The path Puck trod had been built many centuries ago by dwarves who mined gold and gems in the mountain's heart. Most of the tunnels had fallen into ruin, but Fafnir the dragon was known to live in one, blocking the passage through the mountain. 'I can sneak past Fafnir,' Puck thought as he disappered into a tunnel.

Astara couldn't believe Puck could be so silly as to go near the dragon. She didn't want to lose sight of the crown, though, so she followed him into the darkness. It was not long before she began to have bad thoughts about being grabbed by a goblin or a yowie. The tunnel was so dark she also thought she might get lost. She couldn't see Puck any more. She was about to give up and go back when she heard Puck's voice.

'A ruby bright lights the night,' he said gleefully. A red glow lit the tunnel just ahead of Astara and illuminated Puck as he held out the Fairy Queen's gift. 'Aha,' said Puck. 'I am a clever boy.' With his ruby lighting the way he ran on towards the dragon.

Meanwhile, Fafnir was in a very bad mood. He had just caught two goblins raiding his treasure and the last one had given him terrible indigestion. '*Fffffrumfff*,' he belched, and a flame shot out of his nostrils. He rolled onto his back and rubbed his glittering tummy. His scales rang like wind chimes. He waved his tail and scattered a mountain of coins. He closed his diamond-studded eyelids and breathed deeply.

A scent of something familiar, but only dimly remembered, wafted to him on a draft from one of the tunnels. '*Ffff, Ffff, Ffff,*' he sniffed, and opened one eye.

'Faffin ffairy!' he snuffed. 'Fflamin' ffairy with a ffffortune,' he exclaimed, as he caught the smell of the ruby and the crown. 'Treasure,' he smiled, and licked his lips. He slid into a smaller cavern beside the tunnel that brought him the interesting smells.

Puck edged his way to the mouth of the tunnel and peered into Fafnir's lair. It appeared empty and the treasure collected from all over the world lay unguarded. 'My lucky night,' thought Puck. 'Fafnir has gone treasure-hunting.'

He began to tiptoe across a small pile of jewels, when he had the most curious sensation of being lifted off the ground. Then Fafnir's smiling face came into view.

'Fffffinger ffffoood!' roared Fafnir. He removed the crown from Puck's head and tossed it to the floor. In his fright, Puck dropped his bow and arrows and they fell with a sharp *ping!* beside the crown. 'Ruby, please, ffffairy,' said Fafnir, and he held out a paw.

Puck didn't argue. He held out the ruby and Fafnir took it. Fafnir stretched out his wings and stuck the ruby to a small bare spot on his skin. 'Fffffabulous!' he huffed. He rustled all his scales with joy. Then he picked up a large box and popped Puck inside. 'I'll fffffricassee you for breakfffffast,' he added, very pleased with himself.

Once Puck was secure, Fafnir climbed onto a pile of silver, turned around three times, made himself comfortable and began to snore.

Puck spent several minutes pushing at the box's lid, but soon realised it was

tightly fastened. He put his head into his hands. He was very sorry indeed and knew that he only had himself to blame for his predicament. His one hope was that after he was eaten, some brave fairy would find the crown in the dragon's treasure and rescue it. Because of his selfishness all the fairies were in danger. He was deeply ashamed of what he had done, but it was too late to fix it.

Meanwhile, Astara had watched in horror as Fafnir had picked Puck up, and she'd expected him to be swallowed in one bite. She'd breathed a sigh of relief when Fafnir had put Puck in the treasure box. 'What a pickle Puck has put us in,' she thought. She shrank back into the shadows until Fafnir's snores rumbled down the tunnel. Then she peeked back into his lair.

Only a few metres away the crown lay on the floor with Puck's bow and arrows.

The treasure chest that held Puck was near the dragon's tail and a long walk across clattering coins. If the dragon opened one eye he would surely see her. If she tried to save Puck and failed, there would be two fairies for breakfast. 'What am I to do?' she wondered.

She pulled the Fairy Queen's gift from her pocket and gazed at the star sapphire. 'What power does this stone have?' She rubbed the stone between her hands and summoned up strength to rescue Puck.

Fafnir's golden scales rose and fell with each breath as he slept. On his tail was a patch of bare grey–blue skin where some of his scales had fallen off. Astara looked at Puck's bow and arrow and an idea formed in her mind . . .

The Ruler is Crowned

Bravely, Astara tiptoed towards the bow and arrow that lay near Fafnir. As she bent to collect the bow, she discovered she could not see her hands. Not believing her own eyes, she crept over to a large silver shield and peered at her reflection. 'I'm invisible,' she said, and smiled. 'The star sapphire must make you invisible in times of danger!'

Encouraged, Astara took a deep breath, picked up the large shield and carried it very slowly and quietly around the dragon. She placed the shield in front of Fafnir's eyes, then tiptoed back to the bow and arrow and crown. She placed the crown on her head and picked up the weapon. Taking careful aim at the bald spot on Fafnir's rump, Astara fired.

The arrow buried itself in the dragon's flesh and he opened one eye in surprise. The first thing he saw was his own reflection in the shield. With his heart bursting with passion, he leant forward and kissed the dragon before him. Then he began to sing:

'My darling, my love, my one desire,

Your beauty lights my fffffire.

Oh, beauteous creature,

so wondrous, so rare,

Your blazing beauty

is too much to bear.'

With Fafnir totally focussed on himself, Astara went to the chest and opened the lid. Puck peered out in terror, expecting Fafnir to have come for a snack, but found no one there. 'Quickly, Puck . . .' He heard Astara's voice. 'We must run!' Puck felt himself being hauled from the chest. He needed no further prompting, and ran for all he was worth with his invisible friend pulling him along.

Astara headed to the tunnel, which led downhill in the direction of the castle, and as they ran, Fafnir sang. They didn't slow down till they were a long way from the dragon's lair.

'I think we're safe now,' said Astara, trying to catch her breath.

'Is that you, Astara?' asked Puck, still a little shaken. 'How did you become invisible?'

'The magic sapphire – it works when you're in danger. Anyway, here are your weapons.' Puck felt the bow and arrows touch his hand and he took them gratefully. 'Of course, I'm trusting that you won't use them on me again.'

'I'm ashamed,' said Puck, hanging his head. 'You saved my life at risk of your own after I tricked you and left you with the trow. Worse, I've lost the crown. I deserve to be punished.'

'I think being captured by a dragon is punishment enough.'

'The only thing I'm grateful for is that you didn't end up married to that ugly trow.' Puck began to chuckle at the thought. 'You should have seen your face!'

'You should have seen *your* face when you thought I was Fafnir come to eat you!' Astara said sternly.

'Yes, you're quite right.' Puck looked down again, reminded of his shame. 'I have been irresponsible, rude, silly, and I owe you everything. You deserve to be the queen of Faraway Island even though I have lost the crown.'

As Puck spoke, the fairy crown on Astara's head began to glow. Slowly, under its brilliant light, she came into view. Her wings shimmered and her skin glowed pearly bright. Her radiance filled the

tunnel. Puck bowed low. 'My Queen!' he
exclaimed.

With the crown restored, all the fairies
discovered that their powers had returned
and everyone flew home to the castle. A
great celebration was held and all the brave
volunteers told of their adventures in search
of the crown.

Every fairy gave Astara a gift on her
coronation. Eden offered the water bunyip's
cup, but Astara gave it back and told her
she had the responsibility of finding new
spells to heal the sick.

Astara also invited the water bunyip,
Tom Tot, the trow, the wattleman and
Goodewin the gnome-wizard to her
coronation. To each of them she gave a
medal made from Blaize's diamonds. Before
Blaize gave the diamonds to the new
Queen, he sang one of his love spells over

them, so whoever had a diamond was also surrounded with love.

Astara also gave the poor trow and Goodewin extra special gifts for finding the crown.

The fairy friends cooked up a magical cake for the trow, and each fairy gave the cake a blessing. Eden made it taste sweet. Puck made it so it would always grow big again at night, no matter how much the trow ate. And Blaize sang a magic song over it, so whoever ate it was happy all day.

Finally, Astara collected a hair from every fairy who had gone in search of the crown. She wove the hairs into a magical cloth and then made a hat from it for Goodewin the gnome-wizard. The hat had special powers to protect him from bad weather – and lightning.

The Faraway Fairies ™

978 0 7344 1039 9

978 0 7344 1038 2

978 0 7344 1044 3

978 0 7344 1045 0

978 0 7344 1046 7

978 0 7344 1047 4

Win a Faraway Fairies Charm Bracelet★
Can you name the fairies that feature on the front
covers of the first six Faraway Fairies books? Do
you know which symbol each of the six fairies is
linked to? If you know the answers to these
questions, log on to www.farawayfairies.com.au
and enter the online competition. Each person
with a correct entry will receive an exclusive
Faraway Fairies charm bracelet.
Competition ends 31 March 2009★.

Create Your Very Own Faraway Island Scene
The first six Faraway Fairies books include special
cut-out fairies on the inside back cover, which
you can place on a stand★★. Download and print a
special Faraway Island scene from the website,
colour it in and use it as a backdrop to create
your very own magical story with the Faraway
Fairies. There are six cut-out fairies available.
Collect them all!

★While stock lasts. Only one entry per person. Terms and Conditions
apply. See website for full details.
★★If you do not wish to use the fairy in this book, there are other
Faraway Fairies available to print from the website.